Ladybird books are widely available, but in case of difficulty may be ordered by post or telephone from:

Ladybird Books – Cash Sales Department Littlegate Road Paignton Devon TQ3 3BE
Telephone 01803 554761

A catalogue record for this book is available from the British Library

Published by Ladybird Books Ltd Loughborough Leicestershire UK
Ladybird Books Ltd is a subsidiary of the Penguin Group of companies

Top Shelf Ted

by Joan Stimson
illustrated by Kate Simpson

Melanie's Scruff was a bear with ambition. He liked to explore and make discoveries. And now, more than anything in the world, he wanted to climb up to the Top Shelf.

The Top Shelf was the highest point on the bits and pieces rack belonging to Melanie's mum.

If Melanie's mum left her bedroom door open, Scruff could just see the Top Shelf from Melanie's bed.

One day a parcel appeared on the
Top Shelf, which attracted Scruff like a
magnet. It was an ordinary-shaped box.
There was nothing unusual about its size.
But something about this particular parcel
made Scruff's paws itch.

Before long an afternoon arrived which was ideal for shelf climbing.

Melanie's mum had left her bedroom door open. Recently she had re-arranged the books on the lower shelves.

"A perfect pawhold," smiled Scruff.

And now Melanie and Mum had left for the library.

As soon as he heard
the front door close,
Scruff nipped nimbly
across the landing.

He scrambled
up the first two
shelves with ease.

Shelves three and
four were a piece
of cake.

Scruff was just planning
his attempt on the fifth
and final shelf when,
"BRRING! BRRING!"
The phone rang.

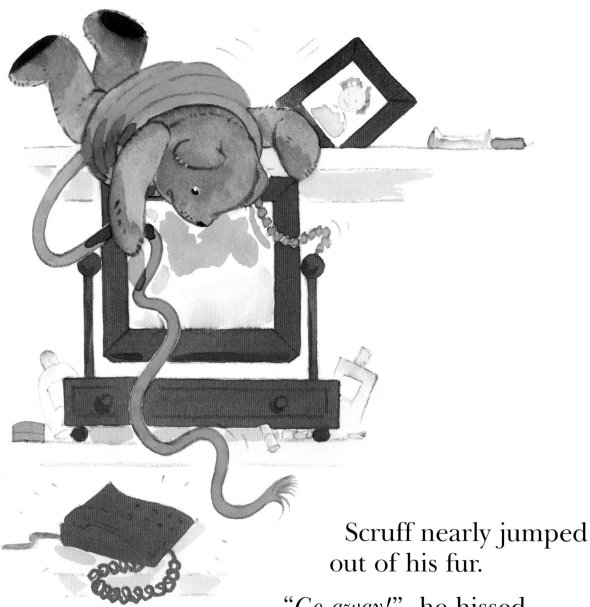

Scruff nearly jumped
out of his fur.

"*Go away!*" he hissed.
"You're making me nervous."

And thankfully, the phone stopped
ringing. Slowly, Scruff began his
countdown.

"*FIVE… FOUR… THREE… TWO…*
WHOOOOSH!"

And with an impressive leap he landed…
on the Top Shelf.

With fumbling paws Scruff attacked the mystery box.

But when, at last, he lifted the lid, he couldn't believe his eyes. Scruff didn't *want* to believe his eyes.

Because inside was a Top Quality, Top Shelf Teddy Bear. Exactly as Scruff had been many hugs and adventures ago.

By the time Melanie and Mum came home, Scruff was flat out on Melanie's bed.

He'd examined his raggedy ear in the mirror…

He'd sighed at the size of the bald patch on his chest…

He'd tried in vain
to wash the paint
from his paws…

But worst of all, he'd
checked out his calendar.

"Just as I thought,"
groaned Scruff.

"It's Melanie's
birthday soon.
*AND THEY'VE
BOUGHT HER A
NEW TEDDY!*"

Later that evening there were rustling noises across the landing. Melanie's mum was wrapping the box from the Top Shelf.

"You *ARE* going to make a little girl happy," she told the Teddy inside.

Melanie's Scruff covered his ears and tried to sleep.

But pictures from the past kept popping into his head.

Melanie's first day at playgroup…

The terrific train ride they'd taken together…

Trampolining on Melanie's new bed…

The time Melanie had held his paw at the Bear Hospital…

"And now that *NEW* Teddy's going to have all the excitement!" sniffed Scruff.

Next morning Melanie's mum was busy and brisk.

"Visitors!" she explained. "One of my old school friends is coming to see us. And I want everyone," she told Melanie and Scruff, "to be on their best behaviour."

Scruff didn't feel like being on his best behaviour. The last thing Scruff wanted was visitors. So all morning he lay on Melanie's bed and sulked.

But after lunch Melanie
came to fetch him.
She had something
to show him.

"Look, Scruff," cried Melanie. "It's
a brand new baby called Miranda.
And Mum's bought her a brand
new Teddy Bear!

Suddenly Scruff felt like a new bear
himself. Tomorrow he might even go
exploring again.

But just for now, he waited for Melanie to tug at his ear. And whisk him outside for their next adventure!

Picture Ladybird

Books for reading aloud with 2 – 6 year olds

The exciting *Picture Ladybird* series includes a wide range
of animal stories, funny rhymes, and real life adventures that are
perfect to read aloud and share at storytime or bedtime.

A whole library of beautiful books for you to collect

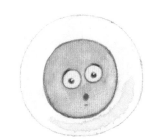

RHYMING STORIES

Easy to follow and great for joining in!

Jasper's Jungle Journey, Val Biro

Shoo Fly, Shoo! Brian Moses

Ten Tall Giraffes, Brian Moses

In Comes the Tide, Valerie King

Toot! Learns to Fly,
Geraldine Taylor & Jill Harker

Who Am I? Judith Nicholls

Fly Eagle, Fly! Jan Pollard

IMAGINATIVE TALES

Mysterious and magical, or just a little shivery

The Star that Fell, Karen Hayles

Wishing Moon, Lesley Harker

Don't Worry William, Christine Morton

This Way Little Badger, Phil McMylor

The Giant Walks, Judith Nicholls

Kelly and the Mermaid, Karen King

FUNNY STORIES

Make storytime good fun!

Benedict Goes to the Beach, Chris Demarest

Bella and Gertie, Geraldine Taylor

Edward Goes Exploring, David Pace

Telephone Ted, Joan Stimson

Top Shelf Ted, Joan Stimson

Helpful Henry, Shen Roddie

What's Wrong with Bertie? Tony Bradman

Bears Can't Fly, Val Biro

Finnigan's Flap, Joan Stimson

REAL LIFE ADVENTURE

Situations to explore and discover

Joe and the Farm Goose,
Geraldine Taylor & Jill Harker

Going to Playgroup,
Geraldine Taylor & Jill Harker

The Great Rabbit Race, Geraldine Taylor

Pushchair Polly, Tony Bradman

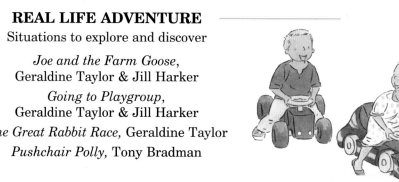